characters created by

lauren child

But I AM an alligator

Grosset & Dunlap

Charlie and Lola ™

Text based on the script written by Bridget Hurst

Illustrations from the TV animation produced by Tiger Aspect

GROSSET & DUNLAP
Published by the Penguin Group
Penguin Group (USA) Inc., 375 Hudson Street, New York, New York 10014, USA
Penguin Group (Canada), 90 Eglinton Avenue East, Suite 700, Toronto, Ontario M4P 2Y3, Canada
(a division of Pearson Penguin Canada Inc.)
Penguin Books Ltd., 80 Strand, London WC2R 0RL, England
Penguin Group Ireland, 25 St. Stephen's Green, Dublin 2, Ireland
(a division of Penguin Books Ltd.)
Penguin Group (Australia), 250 Camberwell Road, Camberwell, Victoria 3124, Australia
(a division of Pearson Australia Group Pty. Ltd.)
Penguin Books India Pvt. Ltd., 11 Community Centre, Panchsheel Park, New Delhi—110 017, India
Penguin Group (NZ), 67 Apollo Drive, Rosedale, North Shore 0745, Auckland, New Zealand
(a division of Pearson New Zealand Ltd.)
Penguin Books (South Africa) (Pty.) Ltd., 24 Sturdee Avenue,
Rosebank, Johannesburg 2196, South Africa

Penguin Books Ltd., Registered Offices: 80 Strand, London WC2R 0RL, England

Library of Congress Cataloging-in-Publication Data is available.

ISBN 978-0-448-44697-4

10 9 8 7 6 5 4 3 2 1

I have this little sister, Lola.
She is small and very funny.
One thing Lola loves is **dressing** up.
"This is my favorite **fancy** dress **costume**
and I'm not ever NEVER taking it off," says Lola.

Then Lola says,
    "Did you know
all-i-gators live in
        swamps and rivers
    where they are very
difficult to see?

That's because they are
        ca-moo-flarged.

    And you know,
alligators lay eggs,
        not babies.

"And sometimes they grow
BIGGER
than even our table!"
says Lola.

"So you see, Charlie,
alligators are really
very interesting.
That's why I am
going to wear my
alligator costume
ALL the time."

So I say,
"ALL the time, Lola?"

And she says,
"Yes, Charlie.
I'm not taking it off ever!
NEVER!"

When mum takes us
shopping, Lola says,
"I want to eat what
all-i-gators eat."

I say,
"I don't think they eat
frozen shrimp, Lola."

But Lola shouts,
"Oh, they absolutely
do, Charlie!
Alligators LOVE
frozen shrimp!"

And I say,
"Shhh, Lola. Everyone's looking at us."

At the park,
Lola is STILL wearing her
        alligator costume.

Marv says,
    "Have you asked her
to take it off?"

So I say,
"A **gazillion**, million times,
        but she says
she is going to
        wear it FOREVER!"

And Marv says,
        "Well, she can't
wear it to **school**, can she?"

And I say, "NO! She
can't wear it to **school**!"

"Of course
I am going to wear it
    to school," says Lola.

And I say,
"I really don't think
    it's such a good idea.
Won't your friends
        think wearing
an alligator costume
        is a bit strange?"

Lola says,
    "No, Charlie.
I think they will all want
    alligator costumes,
too. Especially when
        I do my talk."

So I say,
    "YOUR TALK?"

And Lola says,
        "Yes, Charlie!
We have to do a talk in
        assembly tomorrow.
It's called
            'All About Me.'"

Then I say,
        "But you are
NOT an **alligator**, Lola.
    Don't you think it
        would be better
if you tell the whole
    school about YOU,
dressed as YOU?
        You could tell
    them about . . .

" . . . how you like

drawing . . .

. . . and how you
always hop into bed .

. . . and how
pink milk
      is your
favorite and
   your best."

Lola says,
      "That would not
be very interesting.
            Everybody
already knows I like
      pink milk!"

And so I say,
      "I could help you
with your talk,
            if you like."

But Lola says,
"I do not need any help."

At assembly the next day
Lola says,
"My name is Lola,
and I like **dressing** up.

At the moment,
I like **dressing** up as
an all-i-gator
because it is my most
favorite costume
and it is my best."

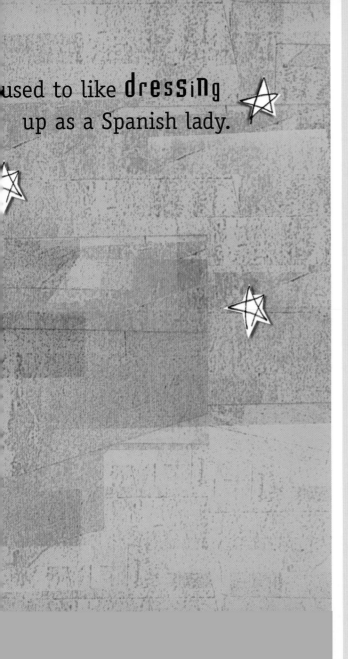

used to like **dressing** up as a Spanish lady.

Or sometimes as a circus person.

But I could also **dress** up as . . .

"... a doctor!

Or a caterpillar ...

. . . who turns into a butterfly."

And the whole school says, "Wow!"

Lola says, "I love dressing up, because I can be whatever I want to be . . . and that is my best."

Everyone cheers.

And I say, "Well done, Lola!"

The next day,
Lola is not an **alligator**.
She has whiskers, pointy ears, and a tail.
Lola says, "Meow!"
And I say, "Oh, no."